Desert Babies

Kathy Darling
Photographs by Tara Darling

Walker & Company
New York

Appreciation is due to The Living Desert of Palm Desert, California—whose celebration of desert life is a model of community involvement. Thanks especially to Susie Kirby for allowing us to photograph animals from the collection.

Thank you to Paul and Brenda Zimmerman for letting us photograph the baby emus bred at Hammercreek Farm, Lititz, Pennsylvania.

To Clark Moorten of Moorten Botanical Gardens in Palm Springs, California, who watches over the baby tortoises that live among his cactuses.

To the Miami Metro Zoo for a bird's-eye view of young vulture life.

To the Animal Kingdom of Bordentown, New Jersey, which allowed us to share their coyote pup.

To Brad, Karen, and Megan Bonar, who have provided a sanctuary for the little caracal we photographed as Black Pine Animal Park in Albion, Indiana.

Really sincere thanks to Clyde Peeling, rattlesnake wrangler extraordinaire, who protected me while I photographed his deadly charges at Reptiland in Allenwood, Pennsylvania.

To the Catskill Game Farm, which has provided an oasis for the baby camels we photographed there.

And to real-life Spidermen, Rob Cherico, chief web surfer of Itchy By Nature in Pompano Beach, Florida, and Frank Somma of New York. We can see how tarantulas like the ones we photographed can get under your skin!

First published in the United States of America in 1997 by Walker Publishing Company, Inc., first paperback edition published in 2002.

Published simultaneously in Canada by Fitzhenry and Whiteside, Markham, Ontario L3R 4T8

For information about permission to reproduce selections from this book, write to Permissions, Walker & Company, 435 Hudson Street, New York, New York 10014

Library of Congress Cataloging-in-Publication Data
Darling, Kathy.
Desert Babies / Kathy Darling; photographs by Tara Darling.
p. cm.
Summary: Photographs and brief text describe a variety of baby animals, some of whom are endangered, who make their homes in the desert.
ISBN 0-8027-8479-8 (hardcover).—ISBN 0-8027-8480-1 (reinforced)
1. Desert animals—Infancy—Juvenile literature. [1. Desert animals. 2. Animals—infancy. 3. Endangered species.] I. Darling, Tara, ill. II. Title.
QL 116.D3 1997
591.909'54—dc20   96-32912
ISBN 0-8027-7533-0 (paperback)   CIP
AC
Map on page 3 and desert and endangered species icons throughout the book by Dennis O'Brien.
Artwork on page 32 by Linda Howard and Elizabeth Sieferd.
Book design by Marva J. Martin.

Visit Walker & Company's Web site at www.walkerbooks.com
Printed in Hong Kong
2 4 6 8 10 9 7 5 3 1

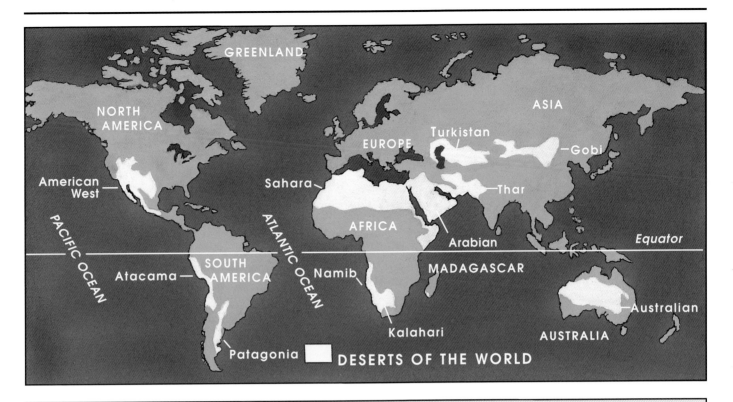

These symbols appear throughout the book and represent the landscapes of the desert that each animal inhabits. For more information about these landscapes turn to "About the Desert" on the last page of the book.

PAN

SANDY

ROCKY

The desert is not the land that nature forgot. It's hot. It's dry. And it's a hard place to make a living. But more than 5,000 species of plants and animals have made desert lands their permanent home.

Join our reading caravan and trek across the burning sands of the Sahara, the pebbly outback of Australia, and the cactus forests of the United States' own Mojave Desert in search of the most adorable babies in the badlands. Of course, in such harsh lands there are bound to be a few tough toddlers too. Come and meet them all.

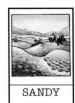

Camel

Some camels have two humps. Others have one. A newborn camel doesn't have a hump at all. It is born without those lumps on its back, which are places for storing not water but fat.

This month-old calf (facing page) is getting fat on its mother's milk. A fat camel isn't fat anywhere but in its hump. It can keep cooler because its whole body isn't wrapped in fat.

The desert's biggest animals, camels are specialists at surviving in hot, dry, dusty places. They have not one but two rows of eyelashes to screen out blowing sand, and special muscles to close ears, nostrils, and lips. Big flat feet prevent the camel from sinking into the dunes.

Camel
(Bactrian Camel)

ENDANGERED
SPECIES

- Baby name: Calf
- Birthplace: Sand
- Birth size: 90 to 100 pounds, 5 feet tall
- Adult size: 1,600 to 1,800 pounds, 7 to 7 1/2 feet tall
- Littermates: None. Twins are possible but not common.
- Favorite food: A baby drinks a gallon of milk every day for a year and a half. After a few months it also begins to nibble on the desert plants its parents eat.
- Parent care: Mother feeds and protects her baby. Camels live in big groups called herds that are led by the oldest females.
- Enemies: Humans
- Home deserts: Gobi and Turkestan in Asia

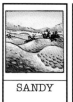

SANDY

ROCKY

PAN

Caracal

This little kitten (facing page) will grow up to be a creep. And a sneak too. Adult caracals (right) hunt by creeping and sneaking.

They are very successful at it. That's because they are also great athletes. If there were Olympics for cats, caracals would win gold medals. This desert lynx, whose strange name means "black ear," is fast and agile enough to snatch a bird right out of the air. A two-week-old kitten like this one is too young for serious athletics, but it will grow up to be the best jumper in the cat family.

Caracal
(KAR-eh-kal)
(Desert Lynx)

ENDANGERED
SPECIES

- Baby name: Kitten
- Birthplace: Hollow tree or underground burrow
- Birth size: 7 ounces
- Adult size: 35 to 55 pounds; 40 inches long plus a 10-inch tail
- Littermates: 1 to 3
- Favorite food: Babies drink milk. Adults eat the meat of birds, mice, and small antelope.
- Parent care: Mother provides total care. Baby stays with mother about a year.
- Enemies: Humans
- Home deserts: Asia, Middle East, and Africa

Gemsbok

Horns! Long, sharp horns. That's the first thing you notice about a gemsbok. Males have them. Females have them. And unlike other baby antelope, newborn gemsbok have them. Of course, they are only baby-sized horns. But gemsbok parents are fierce protectors and will use their big horns to keep their calf safe.

Gemsbok babies, like this two-month-old calf (facing page), are born in the spring so they can eat the green grass that grows only at that time of year.

Are unicorns real? When viewed from the side, the gemsbok appears to have a single horn. Could this antelope that lives in the driest places on Earth be the magical animal of fairy tales and legends?

Gemsbok
(Gemsbok Oryx)

- Baby name: Calf
- Birthplace: No special place
- Birth size: 25 pounds
- Adult size: 450 pounds, 4 feet at shoulder
- Littermates: None
- Favorite food: Babies drink milk for 4 months, then eat grass, plant roots, and melons.
- Parent care: Mother nurses and protects baby. Gemsbok live in groups called herds, and all adults protect young.
- Enemies: Desert lions, hyenas, jackals (babies only), and caracal (babies only)
- Home deserts: Southern Africa

SANDY

Mouse

Egyptian spiny mice have a very short childhood. Most baby mice are born blind, deaf, and naked. Not the spiny mouse. It alone comes into the world with its eyes wide open, able to hear, and wearing a coat of the porcupine-like hairs that give it its name.

In spite of their prickly fur, spiny mice live in groups and love to huddle together between rocks or in earth tunnels they sometimes share with gerbils.

By the time it is seven weeks old, a spiny mouse has grown to full size and is ready to be a mother or father.

Mouse
(Egyptian Spiny Mouse)

- Birthplace: Hole in the ground or crack between rocks
- Birth size: 1/2 ounce
- Adult size: 2 to 3 ounces, 3 inches long (about the same size as a house mouse)
- Littermates: Up to 6
- Favorite food: Babies drink milk for about a week. Then they eat seeds and leaves like their parents.
- Parent care: Mother cares for babies alone. Older females are nurse-helpers at the birth.
- Enemies: Caracal, fennec fox, snakes, big birds
- Home desert: Sahara of northern Africa

SANDY

Quokka

Baby animals are always smaller than their parents. Some are a lot smaller. A newborn quokka, a kangaroo, is 5,000 times smaller than its mother. It's about the size of a grain of rice when it's born.

A tiny baby quokka stays in a pouch on its mother's stomach. When it gets a little bigger, the joey (that's what you call a baby kangaroo) will hop in and out of this handy carriage. Even when it is too big to be carried, like this six-month-old joey (facing page), it will stick its head inside the pouch to take a drink of milk.

Quokka
(KWAH-kuh)
(Short-tailed Kangaroo)

ENDANGERED
SPECIES

- Baby name: Joey
- Birthplace: Under a bush
- Birth size: About as big as a grain of rice
- Adult size: 6 to 8 pounds
- Littermates: None
- Favorite food: Baby drinks milk. Adults eat leaves and grass.
- Parent care: Mother carries baby in pouch. Father does not help.
- Enemies: Feral house cats, foxes, birds of prey
- Home deserts: Mainland and small offshore islands of southwest Australia

Uromastyx

SANDY

If you lived in the Sahara Desert, you could use a spiny-tailed lizard to tell the temperature. The skin of this living thermometer changes color with the weather. When it is cool, a male uromastyx is black. But on a sizzling hot day, which is most of the time in the Sahara, he is a bright yellow color. Females and babies of either sex are a dull brown all the time.

Although uromastyx can stand sand temperatures over 150 degrees Fahrenheit, sometimes the desert is too hot even for them. With powerful claws, a uromastyx can dig a cool underground burrow and block the entrance with a spiny tail that is every bit as dangerous as it looks.

Uromastyx
(YOU-ROW-mass-sticks)
(Spiny-tailed Lizard)

ENDANGERED
SPECIES

- Birthplace: Sandy nest
- Birth size: 3 inches long when it hatches from the egg
- Adult size: 13 ounces, 14 inches long (Males are bigger than females.)
- Littermates: 20 to 30
- Favorite food: Dates, flowers, and plants. Primarily a vegetarian, this lizard occasionally eats insects.
- Parent care: None
- Enemies: Birds of prey, snakes, jackals, caracal
- Home desert: Sahara of northern Africa

ROCKY

SANDY

Coyote

Yip, yip, yip, and yowl is the coyote version of "Home on the Range." At night the little song dog can be heard singing in just about any desert in the American West. The home range of wolves and wild dogs is shrinking in most parts of the world, but the coyote's territory just keeps getting bigger.

Brains are the reason. A toddler like this six-week-old puppy (facing page) is already learning how to outsmart other animals—including humans. The coyote's real home is the desert, and from the salt flats to the snowy high country, it can find food there. But it can also live right in the middle of towns, wiggling its wily way into the backyards of America.

Coyote

- Baby name: Puppy
- Birthplace: Hollow log, burrow, or rock den
- Birth size: 1 pound
- Adult size: 25 to 30 pounds, 20 inches tall
- Littermates: 4 to 9, but 6 is average.
- Favorite food: Puppies drink milk. Adults eat small rodents, birds, and reptiles.
- Parent care: Mother takes complete care of the puppies for the first few weeks. After a month, when pups get teeth, both parents bring food.
- Enemies: Humans, mountain lions, badgers
- Home deserts: Desert and semidesert regions of North and Central America

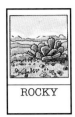

ROCKY

Emu

"Come to Daddy!" calls the father emu when the weather is very hot. He spreads his stubby wings and makes shade for his striped chicks. On cold nights he stretches his wings across the sand and invites the babies to cozy up under his feathers.

His wings aren't any good for flying. That's okay, though. An emu can run faster than any of its enemies. Long legs and tough toes whiz him across the Australian outback at forty miles an hour. That's faster than a horse!

Emu chicks can't run that fast, so their hundred-pound daddy uses his strong legs to protect them. With a loud cry of *"E-moo,"* he delivers a karate kick to anything that is foolish enough to threaten his babies.

Emu
(E-moo)

🌵 Baby name: Chick
🌵 Birthplace: Ground nest made of grass, leaves, bark, or twigs
🌵 Birth size: 1 pound, 6 inches
🌵 Adult size: 120 pounds, 6 feet tall (Females are slightly bigger than males.)
🌵 Littermates: 7 to 9
🌵 Favorite food: Grass, leaves, flowers, fruits, seeds, and some insects. Babies especially like caterpillars and grasshoppers.
🌵 Parent care: Father sits on eggs from several mothers and takes care of chicks for up to 18 months. Mothers do not help.
🌵 Enemies: Dingos, birds of prey, especially buzzards, which break the eggs
🌵 Home desert: Australian outback

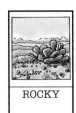

ROCKY

Lemur

For a long time, people thought the spiny deserts of Madagascar were haunted. They heard spooky howls and eerie wails. When they saw pale white forms leaping about, they called them *lemurs*, which means "ghost."

The "ghosts" weren't ghosts at all but beautiful animals that are now called sifaka lemurs. Sifakas, like this adult (right), are great leapers. From a standstill they can jump up to thirty feet sideways, forward, or backward. A newborn sifaka hangs onto its mother's belly fur and gets a wild ride. Bigger babies get to ride piggyback.

Lemur
(Sifaka Lemur)
(see **FAHK** uh **LEE** mer)

ENDANGERED
SPECIES

- Birthplace: Spiny tree or ground
- Birth size: 1 1/2 pounds
- Adult size: 10 pounds, 1 1/2 feet tall with a 2-foot-long tail
- Littermates: None
- Favorite food: Leaves, fruit, and flowers
- Parent care: Baby is cared for by mother only.
- Enemies: Snakes, hawks, and a catlike animal called a fossa
- Home desert: Southern Madagascar, a large island near Africa

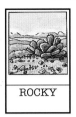

ROCKY

Snake

Rattlesnakes make music but they can't hear their own song. They're deaf.

The little knobs at the end of a rattlesnake's tail are called bells, clickers, buzzers, whirrers, or rattles. But no matter what they are called, people pay attention to the warning noise they make. Rattlesnakes are dangerous. Even newborn rattlers have fangs that are armed with a deadly poison.

With only two rattles, this month-old baby (facing page) can't make much noise. It takes eight buttons to shake up a really loud sound. Rattlesnakes add another button each time they change their skin for a bigger size, and it takes about two years to become a loud musician.

Snake
(Western Diamondback Rattlesnake)

- Birthplace: Mother's den
- Birth size: About an ounce, 8 to 13 inches long
- Adult size: Sometimes over 20 pounds, 5 feet or longer (The record is a 23-pounder that was 6 feet long.)
- Littermates: 3 to 24, although 8 or 10 is more common
- Favorite food: Small animals. Newborn rattlers are big enough to eat a full-grown mouse or a baby bird.
- Parent care: Babies are born alive, not hatched from eggs like most snakes. After birth, mother and father give no care.
- Enemies: Humans, birds of prey—especially the roadrunner—skunks, snake-eating snakes, and pigs
- Home deserts: Mojave, Sonoran, and other places in the American West

Tarantula

Tarantulas are spiders that defend themselves with a most unusual weapon—itching powder. When threatened, they kick special hairs off their rear end at an attacker. Poison in these hairs causes horrible itching if it gets in an animal's eyes or mouth or on naked skin.

This four-month-old spiderling (facing page) doesn't have any of the itchy hairs. It will be a few more months before it has the red color that signals the growth of the fuzzy weapons.

Tarantula
(Mexican Red Knee Tarantula)

- Baby name: Spiderling
- Birthplace: Wherever mother is
- Birth size: 1/3 inch from front to back leg tip
- Adult size: 6 inches from front to back leg tip
- Littermates: 300 to 800
- Favorite food: Babies eat insects; adults eat insects, small lizards, and mice.
- Parent care: Mother carries eggs in a silken case and protects them. Once they hatch, the spiderlings are on their own.
- Enemies: Lizards, snakes, wasps
- Home deserts: Mexico

PAN

Nilgai

Nilgai calves are almost always twins. They look like miniature copies of their mother. The cow and her calves are tawny brown with white markings on the legs and face. These two-month-old babies might not recognize their father. They don't look much like him. A nilgai bull is blue-gray with a black beard and a pair of sharp horns on his head.

If a calf is a male, it will grow up to look like its daddy. When he gets to be six months old, you will be able to see tiny antelope horns beginning to sprout on his head.

Nilgai
(Nil-guy)
(Nilgai Antelope)

- Baby name: Calf
- Birthplace: No special place
- Birth size: 40 to 50 pounds, 2 feet at shoulder
- Adult size: 500 pounds, 4 1/2 feet at shoulder
- Littermates: Usually 1
- Favorite food: Calves drink milk. Adults eat grasses and leaves.
- Parent care: Mother takes complete care of the calf.
- Enemies: Humans and packs of Indian wild dogs called dhole
- Home desert: Thar of Asia

Tortoise

The desert tortoise always carries a bottle of water with it. A special sack under its shell can hold a six-month supply of the life-giving liquid. Half the tortoise's weight is often stored water.

A newborn tortoise's shell is not strong enough to support a very big water sack. It is softer and thinner than your fingernail. Not until seven of the hundred years of its life have gone by will the desert tortoise's shell be tough enough to protect it from its enemies.

This adult desert tortoise (above) lives life in the slow lane even compared to other turtles. For nine months of every year it sleeps underground, surviving on stored food and water.

Tortoise
(American Desert Tortoise)

ENDANGERED
SPECIES

- Baby name: Hatchling
- Birthplace: Eggs are laid in a funnel-shaped nest, often dug near the entrance to the mother's burrow.
- Birth size: Eggs are the size of a Ping Pong ball. The shell of a hatchling measures 2 inches across.
- Adult size: Shell measures up to 14 inches across.
- Littermates: 1 to 11
- Favorite food: Cactus and other desert plants
- Parent care: None
- Enemies: Humans and their automobiles, bobcats, mountain lions, coatimundi, cacomistle, and birds of prey
- Home desert: Mojave in Southwest United States

PAN

Vulture

Vultures eat the most disgusting, yucky things you can imagine. They love decaying meat. Something dead and crawling with worms is, to them, just yummy. One reason they can eat such stinky stuff is because, like most birds, they have no sense of smell. The rotten food is washed down with equally gross drinks. This two-month-old chick (facing page) gets regular deliveries of spit dribbled down its throat!

Flying in lazy circles high over the desert, vultures can spot snacks miles away. With the help of warm air rising off the sand, the searching birds soar for hours without flapping their wings.

Vulture
(Whitebacked Vulture)

- Baby name: Chick
- Birthplace: Huge nest made of twigs and lined with leaves
- Birth size: 3 ounces
- Adult size: 10 pounds, 7-foot wingspan
- Littermates: None
- Favorite food: Meat—fresh or rotten
- Parent care: Both parents sit on the egg and help feed the chick.
- Enemies: Snakes, other birds of prey
- Home deserts: Southern Africa

About the Desert

When you think of deserts, you probably think of sand. But less than 20 percent of the Earth's deserts are sandy. In these lands, the shifting sand is like a grainy sea. Driven by high winds, it moves across the land in waves like a slow-motion ocean. Huge piles of it, called dunes, can rise over a thousand feet from the desert floor.

Another desert landscape is the broken, baked surface called a pan. Made of hard-packed mud or salt, pans are the hottest, driest places on Earth.

Most desert lands, however, are covered with small pebbles or stones. Sometimes called gibber, these rocky places are usually dotted with scrubby plants or cactus and rocks carved into strange shapes by the wind.

A desert is a place where heat, cold, and lack of water all make life difficult. It is also a place where life, with its talent for survival, has responded in marvelous ways. Babies, for instance, are produced only after a rain has fallen and the desert blooms. Desert dwellers are quick to take advantage of these rare times of plenty by storing food and water. Some survive by sleeping during the summer (aestivating) or in the cold months (hibernating). A few even do both. There are animals that don't drink—not ever. And dieters that can stretch a meal for an entire year.

The remarkable babies of the desert can live where we cannot. They can fight and beat the heat, and the cold, and the dry conditions. What they cannot beat is human interference in their fragile ecosystem.

Rain Forest Babies

Kathy Darling

Photographs by Tara Darling

Walker and Company
New York

Thank you, Brad, Karen, and Megan Bonar for letting us photograph the baby Bengal tigers you are raising with such love and care at the Black Pine Animal Park in Albion, Indiana.

And thanks to macaw breeders Pat Galen and Philip Cacciatore for allowing us to photograph their babies.

Text copyright © 1996 by Kathy Darling
Photographs copyright © 1996 by Tara Darling

First published in the United States of America in 1996 by Walker Publishing Company, Inc.; first paperback edition published in 1997.

Published simultaneously in Canada by Thomas Allen & Son Canada, Limited, Markham, Ontario

Library of Congress Cataloging-in-Publication Data
Darling, Kathy.
Rain forest babies / Kathy Darling; photographs by Tara Darling.
p.   cm.
Summary: Photographs and text describe some of the many unique young animals that live in the world's rain forests, including frogs, iguanas, macaws, orangutans, and tigers.
ISBN 0-8027-8411-9 (hardcover).   —ISBN 0-8027-8412-7 (reinforced)
1. Rain forest animals—Juvenile literature. 2. Animals—Infancy—Juvenile literature. [1. Rain forest animals. 2. Animals—Infancy.] I. Darling, Tara, ill. II. Title.
QL112.D37   1996
591.909'52—dc20
95-37738

ISBN 0-8027-7503-9 (pbk.)

Map on page 3 and rain forest icons throughout the book by Dennis O'Brien.
Artwork on page 32 by Linda Howard and Elizabeth Sieferd.

Printed in Hong Kong
2 4 6 8 10 9 7 5 3 1

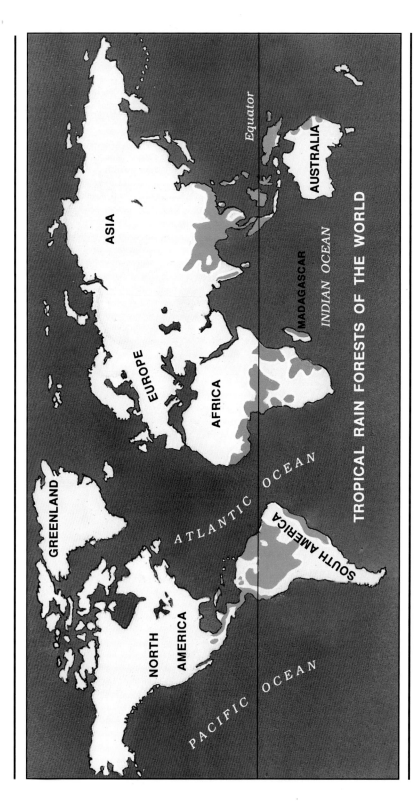

TROPICAL RAIN FORESTS OF THE WORLD

ASIA

EUROPE

AFRICA

AUSTRALIA

MADAGASCAR

GREENLAND

NORTH AMERICA

SOUTH AMERICA

PACIFIC OCEAN

ATLANTIC OCEAN

INDIAN OCEAN

Equator

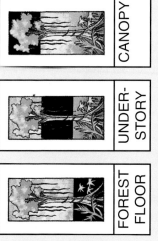

	CANOPY
	UNDER-STORY
	FOREST FLOOR

These symbols appear throughout the book and represent the layer of the rain forest that each animal inhabits. For more information about these layers turn to "About the Rain Forests" on the last page of the book.

The rain forests are Earth's giant nursery. You can find new babies at any time of the year.

Half of all living things on the planet are found in the rain forests. All the tropical rain forests are alike: hot, wet, and green. But each one has animals and plants that belong to it alone.

Come and see what is hatching from the eggs and peeking out of the nests. The rain forests are home to some of the most interesting babies you will ever meet.

Caterpillar

The rain forest is full of bugs. They're creeping and crawling on the vines and bushes. They're flying above the treetops. Look high. Look low. Look anywhere, and you will see insects. They are there even when you can't see them. Whole armies of bugs hide under tree bark or in tunnels beneath the forest floor.

Many insect babies don't look at all like their parents. Caterpillars are young butterflies and moths.

To keep safe, these caterpillars make a little house and pull it around with them. Their mobile homes are made from a rolled-up leaf that is glued with spit. It's hard to believe these ugly wormlike creatures will become beautiful urania moths like the one above. But it happens every day in the rain forest.

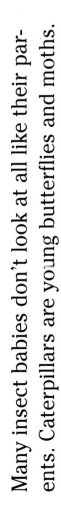

Caterpillar
(Urania Moth)

❖ Birthplace: Hatches from egg laid on a bush
❖ Birth size: About 1/2 inch long
❖ Adult size: Caterpillar is 1 1/2 inches long when ready to become a moth. Wingspan of moth is 5 inches.
❖ Littermates: Hundreds, sometimes thousands
❖ Favorite food: Caterpillar eats leaves; moth drinks sweet or salty liquids.
❖ Parent care: None
❖ Enemies: Birds, frogs, insects, small mammals
❖ Home forest: Central and South America and the island of Madagascar (off the east coast of Africa.)

Elephant

The biggest animal in the rain forest is the elephant. And the biggest baby is the elephant calf. Three hundred pounds at birth, it will become a thousand-pound baby in less than two years. That elephant milk is powerful stuff!

The elephant baby sucks on its trunk like a human baby sucks on its thumb. Trunks are good for other things too: sniffing, putting food and water into the mouth, and playing with sticks and leaves. This calf is part of a big family called a *herd*. There are lots of other elephant babies in the herd, but this calf is only two weeks old and still too little to play with the other babies.

Elephant

(Sumatran Elephant)

* Baby name: Calf
* Birthplace: Forest clearing
* Birth weight: 300 pounds
* Adult weight: Up to 11,000 pounds
* Littermates: None
* Favorite food: Babies drink milk; adults eat leaves and grass.
* Parent care: Baby stays with mother for 10 or more years in a herd of related females.
* Enemies: Tigers, humans
* Home forest: Sumatra (a big island in Asia)

Frog

Frog
(Poison Arrow Frog)

✿ Baby name: Tadpole when young, froglet when older
✿ Birthplace: Hatches from egg on ground. Is carried to a pool of trapped water in the treetops by mother or father.
✿ Birth size: No bigger than a raisin
✿ Adult size: Less than 1 inch long. Can sit on a dime.
✿ Littermates: 2 or 3
✿ Favorite food: Insects, ants, tiny water animals
✿ Parent care: Tadpoles are fed by both parents.
✿ Enemies: Humans and other large animals that may step on them
✿ Home forest: Central and South America and the island of Madagascar

L ook, but don't touch! People who live in the rain forest know to keep away from these beautiful baby frogs. The golden froglets are small, but they are able to take care of themselves. If danger comes, a poison oozes out of their skin. This "sweat" is very deadly. The babies in the picture on the left could kill all the people on earth.

Bright gold is one of the warning colors that poison frogs use. Here are some of the bright patterns they use to say, *Danger! Keep Away.*

Kangaroo

Surprise! There are kangaroos in rain forests. These red-legged pademelons live on the ground. Other kinds hop around in the treetops.

All baby kangaroos have the same name. When they are carried in Mother's pouch, both boy and girl babies are called *joey*. This little one (left) is too big for the pouch, but it will keep close to its mother's side for protection. Don't let Mom's sweet face fool you. She can deliver a kick that would make a karate champion proud.

Kangaroo
(Red-legged Pademelon)

❧ Baby name: Joey
❧ Birthplace: Forest floor
❧ Birth weight: About the same as a grain of rice
❧ Adult weight: 10 pounds
❧ Littermates: None
❧ Favorite food: Babies drink milk; adults eat leaves and grass.
❧ Parent care: Mother carries baby in pouch. Father does not help.
❧ Enemies: Feral house cats, wild dogs, pythons, eagles
❧ Home forest: Australia.

FOREST FLOOR

Tiger

This cute little tiger cub will grow up to be a hundred times bigger than the kitty in your house. It will do a lot of the same things a house cat does, but it will not be able to purr. The tiger is one of the "four who can roar." Three of the roaring cats—the tigers, the leopards, and the jaguars—live in rain forests. Lions, the fourth roarer, sometimes live in forests, but never in rain forests.

Tiger

(Bengal Tiger)

* Baby name: Cub
* Birthplace: Forest clearing
* Birth weight: 2 pounds
* Adult weight: Male Bengal tigers, 400 pounds; females, 250 pounds. Rain forest tigers are the smallest tigers.
* Littermates: 2 or 3
* Favorite food: Babies drink milk; adults eat meat.
* Parent care: Cubs stay with mother for 2 years. Father does not help.
* Enemies: Humans
* Home forest: India and nearby countries in Asia

Chameleon

C hameleons use skin color to send messages to each other. The "color talk" is not something they are born knowing. Like human children, they have to learn their language. Baby chameleons are born pale brown. The only color they can make is green, which helps them hide from enemies. It takes student chameleons about a year before they are able to "read" and "write" in the rainbow colors of an adult like this one (right) from the rain forest of Madagascar.

Chameleon
(Panther Chameleon)

✿ Birthplace: Most hatch from an egg buried in the dirt or leaf litter of the forest floor. Some desert chameleons are born live.

✿ Birth size: There are 128 species of chameleon. The littlest are less than 1 inch long, and the biggest are 2 inches.

✿ Adult size: The smallest species are only as big as a fingernail. Large species can be more than 3 feet long.

✿ Littermates: Up to 100

✿ Favorite food: Insects

✿ Parent care: None

✿ Enemies: Birds, snakes

✿ Home forest: Two-thirds of all species live only on Madagascar. The rest are from Africa and some surrounding areas.

Iguana

B aby iguanas (facing page) look like
ordinary lizards. Big iguanas (above)
look like something from a horror movie.
But things are not always what they seem.

The babies are meat-eating hunters. The
grown-ups are gentle creatures that spend
their days taking sunbaths and nibbling on
leaves and pretty flowers in the rain forests
of Central and South America.

Iguana
(Green Iguana)

❀ Birthplace: Hatches from an egg
buried in sandy soil

❀ Birth size: 10 inches, including
the tail

❀ Adult size: 6 feet

❀ Littermates: As many as 50

❀ Favorite food: Babies eat insects,
leaves, flowers; adults eat leaves
and flowers.

❀ Parent care: None

❀ Enemies: Large lizards, snakes,
jaguars, and smaller, climbing cats

❀ Home forest: Central and South
America.

UNDER-STORY

CANOPY

Lemur

Lemur
(Lepilemur, Ringtailed Lemur, Brown Lemur)

❂ Birthplace: Trees or tree nest
❂ Birth weight: Lepilemurs, 1/2 ounce; ringtailed and browns, 1 ounce
❂ Adult weight: Lepilemurs, 1 pound; ringtailed, 5 pounds; browns, 7 pounds
❂ Littermates: None
❂ Favorite food: Babies drink milk; adults eat fruit, seeds, and leaves.
❂ Parent care: Lepilemurs, ringtailed, and browns are cared for by mothers only.
❂ Enemies: Snakes, hawks, and in some places a catlike animal called a *fossa*
❂ Home forest: The island of Madagascar, near Africa.

Meet the leaping lemurs. Lemurs don't swing through the trees like monkeys. They leap. Mother lemurs leap even when they are carrying their babies.

Lemurs didn't invent piggyback rides, but the babies sure like them. Little ringtailed lemurs ride like jockeys. Brown lemur babies wrap around their mother's waist like a belt. Lepilemurs sit on Mother's back even when they are both in a nest hole.

There are more than thirty kinds of lemurs; they all live on the island of Madagascar, near Africa.

Marmoset

Pygmy marmosets are the smallest monkeys in the world. Their babies are almost always twins. The tiny mother, only four inches long, is not strong enough to carry both babies as she jumps around in the rain forest trees. She has help. Father marmoset is a very loving parent. He washes the twins, cuddles them, plays with them, carries them, and teaches them how to find food.

Marmoset
(Pygmy Marmoset)

- ❖ Birthplace: Treetop
- ❖ Birth weight: 1/2 ounce or less
- ❖ Adult weight: 4 or 5 ounces
- ❖ Littermates: 1 (marmosets are twins)
- ❖ Favorite food: Babies drink milk; adults favor tree sap and insects.
- ❖ Parent care: Father and mother both carry babies for 2 weeks.
- ❖ Enemies: Bigger monkeys, snakes, hawks, eagles, ocelots
- ❖ Home forest: South America

Macaw

Macaw
(Hahn's Macaw, Blue and Gold Macaw)

❖ Baby name: Chick. Called a fledgling when it can fly.

❖ Birthplace: Hatches from egg laid in a tree hole

❖ Birth weight: 1 ounce

❖ Adult size: Hahn's macaw, 1 foot long; blue and gold macaw, 3 feet long

❖ Nest mates: 2

❖ Favorite food: Partly digested fruit and seeds brought by parents

❖ Parent care: Both mother and father feed, protect, and teach the babies for 2 or 3 years.

❖ Enemies: Hawks, snakes, tree-climbing cats

❖ Home forest: Central and South America.

Mother and father macaw have the most beautiful feathers in the forest. But their chicks are naked. Totally naked! Only for a few days, though. Then fluffy "baby feathers" called *down* cover their wrinkly skin. This two-week-old Hahn's macaw (right) is warm in its down coat, but it can't fly with this kind of feather. Down isn't waterproof, either, so the baby macaw won't go far from the nest hole.

At nine weeks, a blue and gold macaw baby (left) already has most of the bright, strong feathers it will need to fly away. But the fledgling is in no hurry to leave its loving parents. Young macaws stay with their family for two or three years.

Monkey

W hen baby monkeys are born, they are strong enough to hold onto their mother's fur. It is not safe for infants to be left alone. Big cats, eagles, wild dogs, snakes, lizards, or other meat-eating animals of the rain forest might kill them. Mothers, older sisters, and aunts watch them closely. These macaques from the Asian rain forest have long tails that make handy leashes for the baby-sitter.

Monkey
(Rhesus Macaque)

❖ Birthplace: Tree or ground
❖ Birth weight: 1/2 pound
❖ Adult weight: 10 to 15 pounds
❖ Littermates: None
❖ Favorite food: Babies drink milk; adults eat fruit, insects, seeds, leaves, and small animals.
❖ Parent care: Mother and the rest of a big family called a *troupe*
❖ Enemies: Tigers, leopards, big snakes, eagles, wild dogs, lizards
❖ Home forest: India, China, Vietnam, and islands in Asia.

Orangutan

Orangutan
(Bornean Orangutan)

❀ Birthplace: Tree nest
❀ Birth weight: 3 1/2 pounds
❀ Adult weight: Males, up to 350 pounds; females, about 150 pounds
❀ Littermates: None
❀ Favorite food: Babies drink milk; adults eat fruit, leaves, and insects.
❀ Parent care: Baby stays with mother for 6 or 7 years. Father does not help.
❀ Enemies: In trees, clouded leopards and big snakes; on ground, tigers
❀ Home forest: Asian islands of Borneo and Sumatra

What's red, weighs three hundred pounds, and swings in trees? Orangutans! Of course, orangutan babies are not that big. But their fathers are. These big red apes are the largest animals that live in trees. Orangutans rarely come down to the ground. Most of their days are spent eating fruits and leaves at the top of the rain forest canopy.

It rains a lot in rain forests. So it is surprising that an animal that lives there doesn't like to get wet. Orangutans hate it. This two-year-old baby (left) is making an umbrella out of a big leaf.

Sloth

The baby sloth likes to take naps. Tip-top naps. In the tallest branches of the rain forest it sleeps away most of the day and all of the night. A snoozing sloth won't fall— even when the wind blows. Long claws wrap around the branches.

Unlike a human baby, the baby sloth never outgrows its need for naps. Even an adult sets aside twenty hours a day for napping. When it's awake, the sloth does everything slowly. It even sneezes in slow motion.

Sloth
(Three-Toed Sloth)

❖ Birthplace: Treetop
❖ Eirth weight: 10 ounces
❖ Adult weight: 7 pounds
❖ Littermates: None
❖ Favorite food: Babies drink milk; adults eat leaves.
❖ Parent care: Mother carries baby for 8 months. Father does not help.
❖ Enemies: Eagles, hawks, jaguars, snakes
❖ Home forest: Central and South America

Sugar Glider

The sugar glider jumps out of trees. Without a parachute . . . and at night. Its target is not the ground but a nearby tree. It leaps from tree to tree to get the sweet sap.

Although it looks like a flying squirrel, the sugar glider is not even a close relative. It is a marsupial—an animal with a pouch. Only as big as a mouse, this baby, four weeks out of the pouch, is already a fearless leaper.

Sugar Glider
(Lesser Sugar Glider)

❖ Birthplace: Nest in a hollow tree
❖ Birth weight: Less than a grain of rice
❖ Adult weight: 2 pounds
❖ Littermates: 1
❖ Favorite food: Babies drink only milk for the first 100 days; adults prefer tree sap and gums, insects.
❖ Parent care: Mother keeps babies in pouch for 70 days, then feeds them in nest for another month. Although gliders live in a colony and share a nest, the mother does all the child-raising chores.
❖ Enemies: Quolls, owls, snakes
❖ Home forest: Australia and New Guinea.

About the Rain Forests

A chain of great gardens circle the earth like a green belt. These are rain forests. In Central and South America, in Africa and Asia, in Australia and on countless tropical islands, giant trees form canopies that stretch for mile upon mile without a break.

Actually, a tropical rain forest is not one but three different worlds—stacked one on top of the other.

The top is called the *canopy*. This is the roof of the rain forest. It is a world of wind and rain and sunlight a hundred or more feet above the ground. The treetops are filled with leaves, flowers, and fruit. Most of the animals live here because this is where the food is.

The middle level is called the *understory*: Bushes, vines, and small trees fight for the sunshine that makes it through the canopy. Here, too, is food and shelter and many animals never leave this level.

On the forest floor is another world. A dark one. Only one percent of the sunlight reaches the ground. On the forest floor are the big animals: elephants, tigers, and people. Millions of them.

This triple world is home to most of the life on this planet. Nine out of every ten kinds of living things we know about live only in rain forests. And some scientists think only about ten percent have been discovered. It is a storehouse of life. Sadly, half of these beautiful gardens have disappeared. Not by magic. But by bulldozer, chain saw, and plow.

See the babies in this book, and look at the treasures we are in danger of losing.